the One, the Only Magnificent Me!

Words by Dan Haseltine

Pictures by Joel Schoon Tanis

Mackinac Island Press

for the love of reading

Text Copyright 2007 by Dan Haseltine
Illustration Copyright 2007 by Joel Schoon Tanis

First Edition

Library of Congress Cataloging-in-Publication Data on file

Haseltine, Dan and Tanis, Joel Schoon
The One, The Only Magnificent Me!

Summary: A disheartened, yet triumphant boy journeys
through the exploration of his own magnificence.

ISBN 978-1-934133-21-7
Fiction

10 9 8 7 6 5 4 3 2 1

A Mackinac Island Press, Inc. publication
Traverse City, Michigan
www.mackinacislandpress.com

Printed in Canada

To Katie, Max and Noah...
the most magnificent characters in my story.
—Dan Haseltine

To Kathy, who lets me dream like a kid.
—Joel Schoon Tanis

I wish…

I wish
I had
feathers.

I wish
I had
wings.

I wish I was covered with prickly things.

I wish I was sort of a blue greenish red, with a hint of bright orange and a spike on my head.

It might be
quite nice
to have a
long
tail,

and a spout on
my back like a
humpback
whale.

Then I would be—
the only one of me,

part porcupine,

fish,

whale,

dragon,

and bee.

And **everyone** **everywhere** would want to come see…

...the one and the only

magnificent me.

But wait!

There's a problem
with all of these
things—

cuz the glue isn't
working to stick on
my wings,

the spikes on my
body make it too
hard to sit, and the
feathers fell off in a
feathery fit.

And that spout
like a whale—
can't really be
done.
I'll just have
to be like—
everyone.

Oh, the stripes! They got tangled,
and won't come untied,

and with all of the dripping, well,
my spots never dried.

I will have to be normal

and sadly just like—

every kid **without**

wings, a tail, or a spike.

What? You say I'm the only kid you see,
who acts quite like, talks quite like,
is quite *like me?*

You mean I don't need
a horn, stripes, or tail?
No **g∞glie** eyes or a
spout like a whale?

I guess you are right!

I just have to be —

TO BE — the one, the only,

magnificent *me!*